Alien Escape

A love letter in eleven dimensions

by Hal Reames

© 2016

Dedication

To Ana Cecilia, June 1, 2016

Acknowledgement

Thank you to WikiMedia for the cover photo

Disclaimer

This is a work of fiction, so don't sue me.

Chapter 1

"It's hot as the devil."

"If I were as skinny as you, I wouldn't complain," said her boss.

She looked over at the CEO, an Alpha--big boned, broad-shouldered, bearded. He was smiling, and that worried her. He didn't usually smile unless he was about to squash something small and helpless, and she was alone with him in the lab.

"We don't have the toxicology report on the drug trial," she told him.

"How are the preliminary findings on subjects?"

"Preliminary."

"I don't know why I let you talk to me like this," he said, placing a meaty hand on her shoulder.

She felt small inside that grip, as if she were a doll that he could toss against the wall in a sudden rage. She decided to humor him: "You indulge me because my timid adherence to the rules saves you from getting fined by the government, which the board of directors wouldn't like."

"Sometimes that's true," he said, and he smirked like some movie star whose name she couldn't remember, someone who appeared commanding and self-confident on the screen. She thought he wanted her to add, "Of course, the final decision is yours, Sir," but she didn't.

When he'd exited the lab, she felt free to go do what she did best, dream up new medicines. But to reach her office, she had to run the gauntlet of the small animal cages.

Her husband sat straight up in bed when heard her scream, "No!"

"The hamsters?" he asked.

She gasped for air. "Yes, I see their eyes--their blind, oozing eyes--and they are screaming when I pass the cage room. They know I am the one who said 'yes.'"

"No, they don't know, and you didn't say, 'yes,'" he reminded her, rolling onto his back, his voice impatient--not with her, but with the Alpha boss who inflicted this on her and on the hamsters. "You wouldn't even sign the request. Remember?"

"I should quit."

"Maybe, but it won't stop him. He needs to build his nephew's resume. To become Director of Research someday, he might need actual experience doing medical research."

"I know. What's wrong with me? Why can't I understand that his future and the future of his family's stock portfolio is more important than a few rodents?"

"Yes, look at the big picture: The kid's not the brightest bulb in the knife drawer, but at least he'll understand what you Beta scientists are talking about, most of the time. The rest of the family has no real background in medicine, chemistry, or pharmacology. They are just business school types, profit seekers."

"They take money from the world and give me a job. I think I should quit and open an animal shelter."

"You must work on your priorities, Love," and he rolled over to face her with a look of complete innocence.

She recognized the look. "Are we now talking about my priorities, or yours?"

"They could be the same."

She rolled over to him, and his long, thin fingers--like those of a pianist--petted her slight shoulder. He held her close and put his face in her hair and inhaled.

"I have to leave that place," she told him.

"Not *this* place, though?"

"No, you're nice. Most people aren't."

In the morning, she was staring into her tablet and sipping coffee when she said offhandedly, "I'm serious about opening an animal shelter."

"Would this be a new job or a second job?" he asked as he put his egg poacher in the microwave."

"Maybe it would in time become a new job."

"Good idea. You're the last person on this doomed planet who should be hearing helpless creatures scream."

She didn't answer except to say, " Is it supposed to rain today?"

"In the northeast, not here."

"I don't remember the last time we had rain."

"It was on our first date. Remember? Ten years ago, I invited you to---"

"---I'm serious."

"It's the worst drought in a hundred years, Love. The reservoirs are dry. The aquifers must be almost empty. It would take centuries to recover from this warming even if we burn zero carbon fuels for the rest of time."

"You said *would,* as if there's an *if* or a *but.*"

"We're not going to recover, Love. The temperatures aren't ever going down. Our sun is on the downside of its lifespan. It's headed for a supernova and will get hotter before it collapses and dies."

"I know. I just don't like to believe it. What are we going to do?"

"Wanna move?" he asked her without looking up.

"Where? No place is safe except the subarctic latitudes, or what used to be subarctic. They're subtropical now. But there's no land for sale up there anyway."

"It's for sale. Everything's for sale at the right price, but only the super-rich Alphas can afford that land."

"The guys who denied it was happening and caused it to continue still managed to hedge their bets, didn't they?"

"I'll get back to you on where we might move," and she knew he really would.

"He wasn't any good at drawing blood!" bellowed the Alpha. He sat at the head of the table, ignoring the current business-school fad of group decision-making. After pausing to let his neck return to its normal size, he said calmly, "We told him to insert the short, glass pipette on inside of eye socket in order to puncture the vein that runs along there. The hamsters survive, and we can determine if the drug is reducing the titre of the virus. But, yes, some go blind, and they aren't pleased by any of this, and they complain. My nephew takes the brunt because they recognize his smell or his footsteps or something about him, and they hate him. And they do stand up on their hind legs, holding their prison bars in front paws and complain--
_"

"They scream," she inserted matter-of-factly.

"Yes, we sacrifice the lower lifeforms for the benefit of the higher life forms, us," he said with a smile. "Half of the planet is tropical now, and this virus is out of control. What's the problem?"

He had no problem at all ignoring a mere hamster's screams, so she answered with an argument he couldn't ignore, "The problem is that this research technique is considered torture, and it violates protocols, and NIID would shut us down if they knew."

He suspected she didn't fear for the company, and she suspected he knew that.

"He could still get credit in his Infectious Disease course if a good phlebotomist took the blood samples," she added.

They both knew that he was only trying to make his nephew look good in front of employees who would someday serve under him when he took over as research director of the company. The young man had been a good athlete and a passable student at his prep school, and one of the few Alphas to be allowed into the hard physics and chemistry classes; but at college he had competed against Betas, nerds like her who could write code and solve calculus problems and understand the smaller dimensions required by M theory. Though no star, he'd found a med school that would take him, and the boss hoped a medical degree would convince them of his competence.

"The hamsters still wouldn't like it," he said.

"No, they wouldn't. This batch will still be blind, and blindness terrifies them so they will squirm and try to bite him, but he will hold them by the back of the neck and insert that pipette between---"

"That's enough!" he bellowed.

"Please let our minutes show my objection to this procedure," she said to the Alpha female taking the minutes. The woman glared back at her from behind heavy makeup. She wore clothing that accentuated her large breasts and hips didn't try to draw attention to her wide jaw and stubby fingers. She had many reasons to hate the Beta who sat across the table with her graceful swan's neck, her violinist's fingers, the eyes of an owl, the gait of a feline, not to mention her clear-thinking brain. The Beta woman recognized the envy in the woman's eyes, but there was nothing she could do to change either of them.

"It's time to test it in flight, Sir," said her husband to his Alpha boss.

"Are you satisfied with the tests in the shop? Do you think it is capable of achieving warp?"

"There's no way to know till we take it outside the solar system and see if we can really stretch space."

"What do you want to do?" asked the man who was the titular head of the entire project.

"I'll take her for a ride, open her up, and see how fast she'll go. If she runs like we hope and doesn't explode, we report to the Committee and see if they are ready to find a planet with a better future than ours, possibly to colonize."

He paused and read the worry on his boss's face. He wouldn't want to change places with the guy. The boss bore the responsibility for the warp engine design, but he didn't really understand how it worked. It was supposed to take explorers to look for another home for humanity, but he knew it was hard for the boss to believe the trip was really necessary. The Alpha's father had been an oil man; and he often quoted his saying, "Those pencil-necked scientists are afraid of their own shadows. If the planet's heating up, we'll find a way to cool it down!" The Beta physicist knew that in his soul the boss felt superior to him, so he hated having to put his career in a nerdy engineer's hands.

The engine's designer watched the Alpha's jaw tighten and told him something that might put his mind at ease. "It's a no-lose test flight for you. If the thing blows up, it'll be my fault and my ass that blows up with it. If it works, imagine the resources we might find. Imagine the money to be made."

"Good sell. You know the board of directors well," said his boss.

"I know it has to pay for itself eventually, like anything."

"You have remarkable common sense for a physicist."

Sitting across the kitchen table from his wife, the physicist knew it was a desperate plan. His type of person had no way to defeat an Alpha if power decided the outcome of the contest. He could score higher on a test, any test except one which measured physical strength; but life wasn't a test of intelligence, not on this Alpha-controlled planet, and that fact had given him the idea.

"Might we all die?" she asked.

"Absolutely," he answered.

It was an answer which told her that he didn't think they had much chance of surviving on the planet much longer anyway.

"Will children go?"

"It's not my decision. What do you think?"

"If we had children, I would take the chance."

"Sad, isn't it?"

"How long will we be cooped up in that ship?"

"It won't seem like so long. We'll take turns in stasis."

"We won't be in stasis together?" She sounded horrified by the idea of being without him, even in her sleep.

"I misspoke. You and I will take turns with other passengers being in stasis. It will feel like a coast to coast train ride--sleeping, eating, playing cards, looking out the window. We'll be together."

"What will we see out the portholes?"

"Bright stripes, mostly. We'll be zooming along inside space that is expanding faster than the speed of light."

"You've done this?"

"Sure, I test-drove the very model. I helped design it, Love."

"Do they know where we're going?"

"They'll set the coordinates, but I have my own ideas; and I really don't want them following us and transplanting this culture to some other world."

"Is the ship ready?"

"I hope so."

"Why don't you give it a longer test drive it till you are sure it's safe for family use."

"Because if it passes a longer test, the wrong families are going to want to take that maiden voyage."

"If it works, can *we* start a family?"

"It has to do more than work. It has to take us to a good place to raise children. This place is not good for you or any children we might have because they would have gentle hearts like you---"

"---Okay, make the proposal," she interrupted. She couldn't stand thinking about her unborn children.

Chapter 2

Months later, a squadron of six, round shuttlecraft revved their anti-gravity engines and prepared for take-off. The slender couple were the last to board. They stood on an elevated platform while a male Alpha in military garb told the assembled government officials how grateful the entire world was for the Captain's contribution to the design and construction of the planet's first vehicle capable of interplanetary space travel and for his willingness to attempt such a voyage, himself, "and of course for his crew of Betas including his lovely wife. It shows great confidence in an interstellar craft he has helped design." His sounded like the voice of God--deep, resonant, sincere.

They shook hands, the physicist's slender hand disappearing into general's massive grip. The couple had only to mount the ramp, turn to wave at the friends who had come to say goodbye, many in tears, and let the incline lift and snap closed.

"Why not send any Alphas to command, General?" asked his aide as the disks lifted until they were almost too small to see and then darted out of sight.

"Because, in all honesty, I don't think they have a snowball's chance in Hell of making it. That's an untried technology, for God's sake. It works on the blackboard, and on one test flight it reached warp speed without blowing up, but hold together long enough to reach another world, an inhabitable world? No chance."

The junior officer glanced his way briefly but didn't stare, so the General answered the unspoken question: "Yes, we have the technology to track them. If they find something useful, we have the second ship, and we can follow them."

"What do you hope they find?"

"An inhabitable planet that isn't overheating. And some lithium would be nice."

With all the shuttles tucked safely away in the first-deck hangar, rocket thrusters took the craft out of the planet's orbit. The crew and their children watched as the solar sail was unfurled.

"Are we going to *sail* to a new home?" asked a child.

"No," his engineer-mother answered, "We don't want to stretch space inside the solar system. It might be disruptive, so this sail will take us above our solar system fast, almost at light speed. Then we'll dowse the sail and start the engines!"

"Did you hear that? She doesn't seem a bit worried," said the Captain.

His wife, now Chief Medical Officer, answered, "She tried to sound optimistic, but only a desperate mother would risk her child's life on such an untried technology."

"And she probably didn't even have any screaming hamsters to deal with."

"No, just the idea of being led into the future by the Alphas. Will they follow us?"

"They know we won't come back if we find an inhabitable planet, so, yes, they'll follow us. We'll have to be ready. No one here is willing to live under their rule again."

"Funny, isn't it? They didn't enslave us physically. We got an education and didn't suffer economically; yet, we found it oppressive."

"An Alpha has a certain genius," he said.

"Are you starting to miss them already? We haven't even left the solar system."

"You, my love, have a genius for empathy. You can sense feelings all around you in every living thing." He saw she was waiting patiently for the *but*. "But, they have a talent for ignoring all of that and focusing on power, on how to get control, how to take advantage and spread their control. The smarter ones can take an ecology course and learn how all things are interdependent, but it has an entirely different meaning to them."

"Do you think they really understand interdependency?"

"Of course they do," he said softly.

"They can't care, can they?"

"It's stronger than indifference. They can't stand being a mere part of the ecosystem. They have to dominate."

"They couldn't let themselves learn from us," she noted.

"I hope we've learned from them?"

"How to dominate?"

"Yes."

"Why?"

"Because they're coming after us," he told her.

As the edge of the solar system approached, families gathered around viewing screens. They didn't know what would happen when the matter-antimatter reactor went online. Some adults silently feared overheating and an explosion. Others didn't want engine failure to strand them in the middle of nowhere and silently hoped it would happen now rather than later.

The children expected an amusement park ride: the plasma would form a warp bubble which would expand space in front of the ship. Then the Captain would stand at the bridge and order, "Engage!" like in the movies, and they would feel a surge, and as they exceeded light speed, stars would turn to streaks.

And that is just what happened.

She watched her husband, the Captain, on the bridge. Totally consumed with checking the readings, he showed no sign of worry or relief. He was just working, doing his job. The chief engineer must have given some kind of warning because the Captain reassured him, "That's to be expected. Keep the pedal down. Warp 1 doesn't get us anyplace."

She didn't get much sleep that night. After a few hours of watching, she took a tour of the ship, seeing it filled with people for the first time. Down the narrow corridors she walked, seeing some families inside their quarters. Others had closed the blinds. She walked through the garden where the plants would give them food and oxygen. The lights had been turned off to let them sleep, and the sprinklers sprayed gently.

As she passed through the aviary, she approached the habitat supervisor, a Chief Master Sergeant, who was carrying sick-looking quail.

"What's wrong with the bird, Chief?" she asked.

"She's come down with something, Doc. I don't think she's gonna make it."

"Poor thing. Let me have a look."

As she placed the hen on a table, the supervisor tell her, "She's lost her balance and started falling down. I think she's come down with something, and I don't want the other birds to catch it, or their eggs, of the passengers." When she continued examining, he increased the pressure: "I know you don't like to see animals fall sick, but I don't think we should waste time, Doc. We don't want an infection to spread."

"She presents us no danger. She has no infection, Chief. I think light speed is wreaking havoc with her navigation system."

"How can we fix that? "

"She is trying to fix on the lights and find a magnetic pole, but she can't, so she is getting nauseated and will stop eating and die."

"We aren't slowing down for a bird!"

"No, I just want you to pull the blinds. That will eliminate the light problem, and then I want to create a magnetic pole in her cage. Could you bring me a six-inch nail, three meters of copper wire, a couple of batteries, and some wire strippers?"

"Much ado about nothing," he grumbled, walking away. "I'll remember that if you get sick," she laughed.

When five minutes had passed with no sign of the Chief, she carried the sick bird to the shop.

"I was just on my way, Doc."

"Sure you were, Chief. As your punishment, take the bird and put her in a box, one almost as big as this table top."

As he walked away, she began to strip the insulation from the wire. Then she wrapped the wire around the nail and attached the battery.

When the Chief returned, she said, "Now, will you walk us back to her cage, and we'll see if this returns her to health and egg production."

When they'd made their trek, they found the Captain at the door of the aviary.

"You're magnetizing a quail hen, Love?"

"I thought it would raise the iron in her blood. What brings you here?"

"Looking for you."

"Well, I think we're done. I'm going to set these lights to come back on in eight hours, and will you put some food in her tube, Chief?"

"How do you put up with her?" muttered the Chief as he passed the Captain on his way out of the aviary.

The Captain felt a surge of anger. He had to resist the urge to punch the man who'd insulted his wife. *How curious*, he thought. *Remove the bigger Alphas, and Beta men start insulting each other, and one Beta husband develops the urge to kill.*

"Hey, Chief, hang on," he said.

"What's up?"

"I'm not saying I always agree with her, but I can say that I always agree with her values and wish I could live by them as well as she does. She is a better person than me, Chief, and a better person than you, too. There's no 'putting up with' going on."

The Chief looked a little stunned. How little conflict there'd been between Betas when the Alphas had all of the responsibility.

The Captain went on, "She complicated your life, I understand that. She does it to me all the time, but when you faced with a choice between a long future and a good future, you zoomed off into the unknown on an untested vessel. If survival is your primary goal, I think you boarded the wrong ship. As long as you're already aboard, you might as well as enjoy the new culture. There is something to be said for respecting the best we have, just as we value the innocent child."

The Chief was paying attention, but no light seemed to have clicked on in his eyes as it would have if there were an Alpha lurking above them both on the hierarchy and providing menace.

"Come talk to me tomorrow, Chief. Let me know if you can forgive my wife for adding to your workload and contradicting your decision. If not, we can find you different work."

That turned the light on. The Chief's eyes got big for a brief second, his jaw tightened, he said, "Yes, Sir," and walked away.

Then end of innocence, thought the Captain. *I hope we wield power more wisely than the Alphas.*

No one would go into stasis for the first week. Then they'd make up a schedule. She knew only that she and her husband would go under together.

He showed more concern about stasis than the warp drive. "Once engines are going, there's not a lot that can go wrong with them," he told her. "Stasis is a different matter." It involved measured doses of nutrients and fluids, continued oxygen administration, the correct frequency and amplitude of brain activity. He didn't want anyone waking up brain damaged.

"What about death? Do you care if we wake up dead?" she teased, but his answer didn't surprise her. He'd just told the Chief the same thing.

Suddenly one morning, every stasis capsule popped open; and for the first time in months, all the passengers were awake at the same time. The ship felt crowded and noisy with everyone poking a head into the corridor and asking, "Are we there yet?" or "Is there a problem?"

She heard his voice on the P.A.: "Good morning, fellow Betas. I have good news and bad news, but not so bad. Nothing to worry about. The good news is that we have arrived at our targeted solar system. That's why we are slowing down. The bad news is that this may be the most challenging part of the voyage, at least for me. As you know, we cannot use the warp drive inside a solar system. The solar sails will not take us *toward* the planets as fast as sunlight sent us *away* from our home planet. So, we have to locate the target planet and then plot a course which allows us to use this sun's light to tack around the planets--it looks like there are eight or nine of them--until we can approach our landing site with the solar 'wind' in our sails. It should be fun. I'll keep you informed."

She tried to focus on her duties while they tacked back and forth, each changing in direction causing passengers to fall against walls and grab for a hand-hold. Those duties included talking to the animals in the garden, reading to the children, and administering antivirals to those who'd caught a cold. She knew her job protecting their health would grow more complicated once they lowered the ship's gangplank to a new world of infections.

But when they'd arrived far above the blue planet, the main hatch wouldn't immediately open to this alien world. First, they had to take readings of the air and water. Could they breathe down there? Could they hydrate? And what germs were in the air? Soil samples would have to wait till they sent a landing party, if they ever would.

Passengers gathered around the screens to see the pretty ball below. More than half was blue. "That's water," the parents explained. "We don't know if it's drinkable. The white at the top and bottom must be snow."

"The puffs must be clouds," guessed a child.

Then the readings started arriving: a layer of ozone for protection, enough oxygen, more than at home. That brought cheers to two generations that had been short of breath at home.

"Cyanide levels in the air, okay," brought cheers.

"Carbon monoxide, okay," more cheers.

"Ph of the water: not too basic, not too acidic," so , the natives weren't suffering from acid rain.

"Air temperature range: 55 to -85, most safely in the middle." The mother ship exploded in celebration that the planet wasn't overheating.

"Are they even industrialized?" someone asked.

"Is there even a *they*?" came an answer and the realization that they knew nothing about possible inhabitants. On the viewer came the sight of sixteen crewmen dressed in flight suits boarding one of four shuttles. Silence fell over the passengers. Everything hung in the balance. Nothing else mattered--not the water, the air, the temperature--if the creatures below proved incompatible with the life they wanted to live, if it would be a life of constant strife between their race and the men below.

Chapter 3

It was back in 1947, Earth time, when humans were given good reason to suspect they weren't alone in the universe. The visitors weren't shy. Radar picked up four aircraft behaving strangely over Los Alamos, New Mexico, home of the Jet Propulsion Laboratory. Jets scrambled and took chase, though it wasn't much of a chase.

They took directions from radar and the nearby base: "Continue due south."

"What's there speed?"

"Zero. They seem to be hovering. Now one has gone up, one east, one west, and the other straight down. Good luck."

"Whaddya mean, 'good luck'? What do we do?"

"Command says to follow the one headed down. He may be landing."

"Whose are they?"

"I hope they're ours because if they're Russian, we're in deep shit. We don't have anything that can maneuver like that or reach the altitude of the one that went up."

The Americans wouldn't find out till a few years later that the Russians *were* interested in the activities at Los Alamos. They were spying on the labs to learn how to make an atomic bomb, but not by air. Julius Rosenberg's brother-in-law would give them what they needed at the cost of Rosenberg's life and that of his wife.

Not knowing of this threat, the squadron of XP-84 fighters followed the unidentified object headed down near the town of Roswell, New Mexico. As they neared Roswell, the squadron observed a yellowish-white, circular object hovering at about 10,000 feet. As they approached, it veered at a sharp angle to the east at only about 200 mph. In moments, the other three discs appeared.

"How fast are they coming," the pilot asked radar.

"My guess is at least 1700 mph."

"Inform command," radioed the pilot, wondering what aircraft could reach such a speed. Then the other three saucers decelerated at an impossible rate and hovered above the fourth disc.

"No human could survive that deceleration," said the pilot into his radio.

The three jets passed by the hovering disc and veered right, left, and up to make another pass. As they approached, the pilot of the lowest disc dipped a little too far, scraping the farmland below.

As far as the military jets could tell, the three other discs made no response. The jet pilots could not see three surviving crew being electronically transported to the three other discs. But the pilot of the fourth craft had died and was not transportable. Aware the pilot had died, the Captain of the mother ship ordered the two intact shuttles to return to the ship. One was ordered to observe from a higher altitude. In a matter of minutes, land forces from the Army's branch of the air forces arrived at the wreckage.

That night on the mother ship, the team was preparing to review the crash. When the Captain entered the flight deck, he announced, "We have to know why that shuttle went down. Check data flow from his altimeter and the gravity calculations, AI."

"They are identical to the other three craft, Captain, but he was the only one that descended, so let me see his last reading. No, according to his instruments, he crashed at zero altitude."

"So why did he lose altitude?"

"We can't check his engine."

"No, so check all three of the other engines for signs that the superconductors are experiencing electromigration," said the Captain.

"The current looks normal," said AI.

"I'd like a visual inspection too, Chief."

"Give me a few minutes, Captain."

As they waited, the Captain thought aloud, "I wonder if they will know we are from another planet."

"I'm pretty sure they will, Sir."

"What haven't you told me?"

"They look more like the Alphas than us," explained the pilot of the shuttle that had stayed to observe.

"How so?"

"Tall, thick, hairy, and not grey like us."

"Don't judge them yet. Let's do more reconnaissance, find out what's going on here before we contact them."

Over the intercom, the Chief Engineer reported, "No problems found with any of the superconductors, Captain. What do you think?"

"Pilot Error," said the Captain. "That we can fix."

The following day, July 8, 1947, the *Roswell Daily Record* reported, "RAAF (Roswell Army Air Field) Captures Flying Saucer on Ranch in Roswell Region."

The U.S. government claimed that a weather balloon had crashed on the Foster ranch on June 14, 1947, and the Foster's foreman, a man named Brazel, asserted that he was in the area and found some wreckage--nothing much, just some foil, rubber, and wood scraps.

The next morning at about 8.00 a.m., three highway department employees near Yuma, Arizona reported three silvery disks flying northeast at high altitude. At around 9.30 a.m., four soldiers at a nearby base reported two circular objects flying into the horizon in tight circles. Later, at about noon at nearby Rogers Dry Lake test range, two technicians observed a silvery object hovering at about 20,000 feet for about a minute and a half.

Finally, at about 9.00 p.m. that evening, a P-51 pilot twice attempted to intercept what he would describe as a flat light-reflecting object, though he was unable to reach its altitude, so it was somewhere above 20,000 feet.

The following day, the officers met in the conference room. They sat at a round table, not rectangular and not as tall as those built for the Alphas on their home planet. This table accommodated their size and shape and decision-making style, and they sat smiling and joking, not even thinking about why they felt so contented here in the middle of nowhere. The Chief Medical Officer noticed, though.

She sat in a strapped T-shirt, exposing her upper back. Her husband, the Captain, passed behind her and saw the patch of familiar silvery skin between her shoulder blades. Unable to resist, he bent over and rested his cheek on this warm spot and inhaled. The other officers smiled and went on with their conversations, enjoying the informality they could share in the company of fellow Betas.

Finally, the chief engineer asked her, "Who is that man you have attached to your back this morning?"

"What man?" she asked. She looked around the table and shook her head almost imperceptibly, as if to say, "I'm not responsible for him."

He raised his face and said, "I need fifteen more minutes of sleep. Report on the functioning of the engines, Chief."

Since the engines showed no problems, they next turned to intelligence gathered on the creatures below. Somewhere on the planet, they guessed, their hosts were holding a similar conference about them.

"Have you translated the communications from the nation immediately below us?"

"Yes, it was the right place to visit. It has become the dominant nation, but only recently. They just completed a major war that has left only this nation undamaged among the participants. The world's most populous country is primed for a revolution, it seems; but that worries them less than their rivalry with a former ally which seems to be spying hard to uncover the secret to their nuclear bomb."

"Did they employ it during the war?"

"Yes, twice."

"Did we actually travel in space or just back in our own timeline?" asked the Chief Medical Officer, the female to which the Captain's cheek had recently been attached. Then, "What are they using as fuel?"

"Carbon fuels. We sent a team to their southern pole. Carbon dioxide had been rising for more than a century, but it's accelerated recently. I find no evidence that they are aware of the danger."

"We should alert them!" suggested a communications expert.

The ship's doctor said, "If we can find someone who can hear the message. These are tribes warring for dominance. Mutual survival is not their priority. They are overheating their planet for profit and control-- sounds familiar."

"Technologically, they are behind us but progressing. From what we can tell, only about one-third of the species engage in any semblance of abstract reasoning. With a limited capacity to understand the forces at work, few give any thought to long-term consequences."

"With so many threats, how do they avoid anxiety?"

"Many of them just rely on hope, an emotion which calms them. Often this hope is based on religious beliefs. Strangely, we looked at their belief systems and found the most vociferous believers to be driven by adrenaline."

"How so?" she asked.

"Their writings describe various deities or prophets who have walked among them. Even though most of these preached love, when faced with a nonbeliever, the followers of these sages react as if a difference of opinion were an attack, and they become either frightened or angry, both being driven by the adrenaline's effect on one particular part of the brain, which they call the amygdala."

"How can such a system lead to rational decision making."

"They just dropped nuclear bombs on two cities full of civilians, so I don't think it's working too well."

"Do their religions preach mass killing of fellow humans?"

The commander looked to the communications director, who answered, "Not that I found."

"How did their warring leaders come to power?"

"Different ways. Of the main leaders in the recent war, On the instigating side, two were elected and one was a hereditary emperor. These two elected leaders were both bellicose speakers who convinced their electorate that they had to attack others to attain power, wealth, and, one would guess, security. Two on the victorious side were elected and one was a dictator who came to power via force. "

"Even an complete idiot could win one of their elections if he talked tough enough," scoffed the chief of security, and everyone laughed along as if it were a joke.

"Only if the enemy were external," replied Communications officer. He reminded them of his own world's history, "If he talks tough about countrymen, he will divide his support."

"Unless they were some despised minority."

"Example," requested the Captain.

"One leader on the losing side of their war focused on a hereditary-based religious minority."

"Who were they?"

"They're called Jews, and his government killed millions of them."

"They sound quite different from us," insisted Security.

"Maybe from us here in this room, but in some ways it sounds like our home planet, with two very different kinds of people, except they are of the same species and you can't tell which is which by looking. Humans might be either aggressive or cooperative and respectful of differences, but to us the two types are physically indistinguishable."

"I think we need to talk to the human version of us. Can you identify one of the Jews for me?"

"I'll try."

Chapter 4

The shuttle dropped down from the mothership and sliced into the atmosphere above Roswell, then veered east and within an hour was approaching Princeton, New Jersey. The Captain and his Chief Medical officer looked out the portholes as they made a pass over New York city. She gasped quietly when she caught sight of all the lights.

"I wanted to see it close up," he told her.

They then swung southwest and hovered over a two-story, wood-frame house.

"Tell me again why we have to climb down this wiggly rope ladder, my dear physicist husband."

"Because our transporters can capture all of the information needed to reproduce a black hole, or a person, in two dimensions; but unless you want to go through life as a flat picture, you need a receiver which can reconstruct the image in three dimensions."

"I knew that," she said. "You go first, and catch me if I fall!"

After travelling millions of miles by expanding space, itself, they landed on Earth by flinging a rope ladder into a backyard in Princeton, New Jersey, where the two visitors knocked at the back door.

A housekeeper answered the door. "Oh, my," she called out. "Professor, I believe you have guests."

"Who, at this hour, with no appointment?" he yelled from his study.

"I think you will want to receive these guests, Professor. I suspect they've come a long way." By now she stood with the two Betas at the study door and tapped on the door frame.

The professor turned, stared a moment, then quietly said, "Yes, please come in. This is a surprise, but a pleasant one. Do you have trouble understanding my accent?"

She smiled at the small man with the wild hair, her little mouth and big eyes making her look timid, but she sounded confident as she spoke into her microphone, "I can hear you fine now that I've adjusted my earpiece."

"A translator? How wonderful!" he said.

"And this is my husband and commanding officer, for the time being." They approached him and took his hand when he extended it first to her and then to her husband.

"Enjoy your rank while you can, Sir. You'll be demoted when you return home."

"Gladly," he said. "I imagine you have some questions for us, but we have some questions about mankind, too."

"As do I," said the earth's greatest physicist and recently a failed opponent of the atomic bomb.

They talked far into the night about the strife on both of their planets, about human nature, about expanding space to travel faster than the speed of light without violating the Professor's theory. This pleased him greatly. The earthling was less euphoric when he heard the suggestion that he shouldn't give up on quantum mechanics.

"It only seems like God is playing dice because the scale is so small and the speeds are so fast. Whenever the math works, you can't ignore it," advised his colleague from elsewhere.

"The idea that anything mathematically possible must someday happen is preposterous."

"Yes, it assumes an infinity of time, but we almost certainly don't have an infinity," hinted the Beta physicist. "When you see what our universe is doing, you'll see that it doesn't have infinite time."

"'Our' universe? Do you think there may be other others?"

"If it can happen once, why not over and over and elsewhere in space-time? Once you work out the math and understand black holes, it'll all make sense."

"Not this quantum spookiness. That'll never make sense."

"It's only spooky if you think of space as empty and straightforward."

"How does entanglement work, then?" The earthling sounded both excited and resentful.

"I can only give you hints."

"Why?"

"We have pledged not to jump-start your science."

"We've *already* started!"

"Of course you have, but I mean that we can't boost it to the next level."

"So what other hint can you let out of the cat's bag?"

"Those spooky distances aren't as large as they seem from our point of view, not if you understand the mechanics of it all."

"What do you mean, the 'distances aren't as large as they appear?"

"Strange as it may seem, from some perspectives space is not as vast as it appears in our four dimensions. From the point of view of entangled particles, for example, the distance between them may actually be much closer than it appears."

"Through a dimension in which light can't travel!" he trumpeted.

"I hadn't thought of it in those words, but yes."

Then the earthling heard what he'd said and asked, "You said 'Dimensions.' Then I used the word, myself. But how can we talk about more than three dimensional space and time?"

"I'm afraid humans need more data, and you're looking, so it'll come, but maybe not in your lifetime. You are right that the spookiness can't be what it seems. Entanglement happens, and it's wonderful, but it isn't magical. Like any magic show, the trick is an illusion based on the fact that you don't yet see the physical reality."

"My equations for gravity work. They predicted the bending of space-time."

"Good for you, but what causes gravity to work? You call it a force, but what mechanism pulls one object to another? You are doing great at the math, but don't assume you understand the physics just because the math works."

"But you just warned me that if the math works, I can't ignore it just because it doesn't yet make sense."

"That's true too. How can I explain without explaining? Just remember, nothing is empty. It might not have matter in it or what you recognize and can detect as energy, but it isn't empty."

"You shouldn't have told him that," she whispered.

"So, we could use space itself to propel us?"

"You're a quick study."

"Take me with you! I want to learn what you know."

"We can't remove this world's most crucial physicist. By the way," he said, trying to change the subject, "We've been monitoring on your news. Congratulations on the nation of Israel."

"It isn't a nation yet. Israel and Palestine were named 'states,' whatever that means. How they are going to house and feed the world's Jews in that desert, I don't know."

The two visitors exchanged a glance that said, "Go for it," and she reassured the Professor that with all that sunlight, they should be able to generate plenty of electricity, enough to power a desalination plant that forces water through a membrane which removes the salt; and in a final good-will gesture, they showed him their computerized translators. "Microcircuitry," they explained when he looked at a chip. "Lithium battery," they admitted when he touched a battery.

"Lithium. Yes, that makes sense. But what could work as a anode?"

They did not answer.

"We must seem quite primitive to you," he said sadly, "the idea of burning things up for power."

"Despite our interstellar travel, our politics have not advanced much beyond yours, and we burned carbon for far too long and wiped out many habitats that helped protect the air and water, and those are the reasons we are leaving that world."

"But are you staying here?"

The couple exchanged a look. They hadn't officially discussed it with the crew. She said, "We don't know yet, but we aren't returning to our home world. At least you have defeated your Nazis. We can't oppose our oppressors with force."

"Are they open to negotiation?"

"Oh, they love to make deals, but they don't make concessions. They benefit from our talents, just as governments here benefit from your discoveries---"

"---but don't listen to me when I advised against exploding the nuclear bombs on Japan. So, this is your Exodus, and perhaps Earth could be your Promised Land. There is someone you must meet before you leave. I will arrange a meeting." He looked at his calendar and said, "for January 30, 1948. I happen to know he will be in New Delhi on that day."

"Who is this person?"

"His name is Mahatma Gandhi."

"My translator tells me that his name means 'great soul.'"

"And he is. He is. His voice speaks for the best that is in us."

"Then we will go listen to his voice," she said, and her husband nodded in agreement.

When he thought they were preparing to leave, the Captain heard his wife clear her throat, and he smiled at the surprise that would come.

"Professor, may I ask you a question unrelated to physics and politics?"

"Certainly, Doctor."

"I saw a creature as we were approaching your door, and I think I frightened it to death."

"Why?"

"I just looked at it, and it fell over as if it had died, and it even began to smell as if it had immediately begun to decompose."

"Yes, I think I know the creature," he said. "It likes to eat from the cat's dish. The cat doesn't seem to mind. They take turns. Come, I'll show you,"said Professor the Professor as he walked them to the side door.

"It isn't dead?"

"Take a peek," he whispered

"'*Peek*, a quick look,' she translated, "so I shouldn't stare." Stepping out the door, she whispered, "What is it?"

"It is an opossum, *die frau*, not evolution's greatest masterpiece, but it survives. As you noticed, they don't seem very appetizing. This one is still a juvenile."

"Is it a male or a female?"

The professor thought how hard it was to tell these two husband and wife aliens apart except for their hair, and he smiled. "I haven't studied the problem," he told her.

"Mmm, may I talk with her?"

"She's not much of a conversationalist."

"Would she eat one of those fruits I saw in the bowl on the table?"

"You're welcome to one."

She brought an apple from inside and walked to the farthest edge of the concrete slab at the back door. Her eyes on the opossum, she bit a piece off, and placed it as close to the creature as she could reach. Then she bit off another and tossed it a little closer, and another, and another, until the fifth piece landed beside the cat's dish.

Without turning to look at her, the 'possum picked up the apple piece with both hands and brought it to his mouth. Then he lost interest in the cat food and one piece at a time ate his way toward her until he stood just out of her reach. She took another bite, stretched her arms toward the opossum and let the morsel slide between her thin, grey fingers onto the deck. She left her hand there as it ate. Then she slowly retracted it, sliced off another piece, reached out a closed hand once more, and opened her fingers. The opossum picked the piece from her open palm. She felt a gentle tickle from its fingers but left her palm there a moment while it took another bite. This time she stretched her open palm directly to his mouth. He places both paws on her hand and took the piece in its mouth with the sweep of a tongue. They exchanged a look.

"What does it eat when no one leaves cat food?" asks the woman.

"Bugs, garbage and dead things."

"May I adopt it and take it with us?"

Her husband saw tears in the earthling's eyes.

"She is too good for this planet," said the Professor. "If you stay, I hope you can find safety, if there is such a thing in this universe."

"Whether we stay or go, I fear that we are just the first wave. I hope we have hidden our footprints well enough, but if our dominant species finds its way here, they will bring weapons and will want your wonderful water, clean air, and plentiful empty land."

"They sound familiar."

"Have you been visited already?" she asked..

"Maybe, but probably not for several thousand years. There are many hints. But when I said that they sound familiar, I was referring to that group which started our great war. They emerged from the world's greatest culture, tried to conquer the planet, slaughtered millions of my fellow Jews, and was finally bombed into submission."

"We just missed them. How fortunate, but we brought no weapons," said the immunologist.

"Brought no weapons." Sigh. "I wish I'd met you sooner. How can you explain your peacefulness?"

She answered, "I suspect we have higher levels of oxytocin than most humans."

"What is oxytocin?" asked the Professor.

"It is the chemical that is released in the mother on your planet. The females of my race have constantly high levels, so they are drawn to helpless creatures, and the mammals usually respond just as this opossum has responded."

"The other race is different?"

"Yes, their females are transformed by childbirth. Then they become devoted to the baby and are gentle with it, but their mothering reaction is very specific to the infant. They aren't any gentler with anyone else, including their older children."

"I don't sense much aggression from you either," he said to her husband.

"No, we must learn how to defend ourselves, and I can, but it would be a bloodless fight."

"How so?"

"My blood wouldn't boil, and my enemy's would barely spill."

"How would you defend yourself without hurting him?"

"I can't say my enemy would escape without injury, but we don't fight to dominate or destroy because it gives us no excitement. It doesn't involve rage, just targets. Unlike the Alphas, we really don't much like big surges of adrenaline. The Alphas feel it as pleasure. We don't."

"I fear my species is more like your Alphas than you. Do you even belong the same species as the Alphas?"

"Maybe long ago, but no longer. We cannot interbreed--very different epigenetics."

"I haven't heard the term," said the Earth's greatest mind, "but the word would suggest that not only have you understood the chemistry of genetics, but you have also discovered that variations in gene expression may be influenced by another level of chemical intervention."

"Yes, how quickly you understand. It important that our Alphas not find you. With men like you, your species has the potential for a wonderful future."

"Good or bad, I wouldn't use me as your sample. No one has ever accused me of being typical in any way. You will like Ghandi. Let me set up a meeting for you."

Chapter 5

The following month, at around 5:00 on January 30 of the new year, a disc dropped out of the sky over New Delhi, India. While the pilot steered, the Captain focussed his telescope on the steps outside the Birla House, scanned for Gandhi, and spotted him surrounded by some young women. He watched a man approach, say something, push a girl aside, and fire a semi-automatic pistol. Seeing Gandhi sag, he aborted his descent:

"We can't stay here," he says.

She studied his face. "Maybe we can help," she said.

"I don't think we can," he told her. "I saw something as we flew over, something that made me think of hamsters. Instead of Gandhi, let me just show you a creature I've been studying."

He took the controls and steered the shuttle to the edge of a forest. No one was in sight, so he landed the shuttle and conducted a scan. "A family is headed this way."

"Will we frighten them?"

He realized her question had captured the predicament they faced when introducing themselves to the humans--coming with different ideas, different appearance, advanced knowledge that threatened what these aggressive mammals believed. "Let's step out of the shuttle and see."

In moments, an elephant emerged from the forest and swung her trunk into the grass, gathering a bundle.

"Oh, look at the nose! It works like a hand," she laughed.

The mother elephant heard her laughter and looked more closely in the direction of the shuttle as her offspring joined her in the clearing.

"Does she know what this is?"

"She may have seen a helicopter. Hunters use them."

Mention of hunters unleashed a flood of questions: "Hunters? Do they eat these creatures? Why would they? Is there not enough food? Who cares for the little ones if the mother is killed? Well, the offspring isn't so little, but she's still just a baby. Are they mammals?

Of course they are." Worry pulled her face into a frown, but not worry for herself.

She gathered still-green grasses into a bunch and wobbled forward on her thin legs, her head down and her offering extended. Her husband watched her . *We are such a frail species. I hope this elephant will see her for what she is. She will certainly not mistake her for a human. I hope elephants are as intelligent as I'm told.*

His wife offered the grasses to the mother elephant, and the calf drew close. The mother did not take the grasses, did not shoo the baby away. She simply watched as this alien creature turned and fed her child. When the calf bumped against the woman, the mother nudged her child away with her trunk and protected the alien. The husband watched the elephant's eyes staring down with no expression he could read. His wife patted the forehead of the baby, stared up at the mother, and sang a verse of a nursery rhyme in their language. Then she turned to leave.

Once in the shuttle, she thanked him and asked, "Looking into her eyes is like seeing this world's memories, so old, so wise. That was very generous of her. She doesn't trust humans much, but she liked me and knew I meant them no harm. But why did you show me these creatures?"

"I wanted you to have a good memory of this world. We must leave. If we stay, it will break your heart."

"Maybe I don't need to know why we aborted the meeting with this Gandhi."

The entire crew was gathered in the garden at the Captain's request. He watched them find their places, friends among friends, families carrying toys for their children, couples--some happy, some obviously feeling the strain of weeks spent aboard, not yet having had their chance to site-see in one of the shuttles.

"Everybody's going to have a look at this planet," the Captain said. "I'm especially fond of the Amazon trip and the penguins on the South Pole." He heard "yays" from the children and their parents.

"Will we meet the earthlings?" asked a little girl.

He waited until the jabbering stopped and everyone realized he hadn't said, "Yes, of course."

"I'm afraid the most beautiful things about this planet are the landscape and the animals. There are probably some earthlings who would be kind and welcoming. We met one, and we made a video of him which we will show you in a few minutes."

When the children began to jabber again in excitement, the parents shushed them, realizing that he had more to say and sensing that it wasn't good news.

"Earth is the destination set for us by Alpha command, and that means they will be arriving soon. We don't have much time because 'soon' will happen faster for them than for us because they will be coming faster than light speed. You all know how that works," and they all nodded, even the preschoolers. "That's the bad news, but the good news is that we couldn't stay here anyway. This is a world controlled by men much like our Alphas, but they look just like the humans who are more like us, so you can't tell the safe earthlings from the dangerous ones. It's a shame," said the Captain. "Some have wonderful minds and good souls; yet from the same species came men as domineering and exploiting as our Alphas. They have a brain that evolved to ignore its own compassion and spend its energy plotting for control, for dominance, defeating human enemies instead of tending the garden they've inherited from the cosmos."

She surveyed the audience and saw disappointment and frustration on the faces. They needed an example that would move them in the way Gandhi's murder moved her husband, and she had one.

"May I show everybody some of the animals from earth, Dear?" she asked.

He didn't see how cute animal pictures were going to persuade his fellow travelers, but he said, "Sure," and sat down.

"We can't take representatives of all the wonderful species, certainly not the whales and dolphins and elephants, not even the birds that can talk and the apes that could if they were taught to use sign language. But we have taken this opossum, Carlos---"

"---perhaps the dumbest, most disgusting creature on the planet," the Captain interrupted, "and I do not yet know why we are taking Carlos."

She just smiled, and the assembled laughed and knew they'd eventually find out why.

"We have left behind many beings who are much like us, much like us. They may ultimately preserve the planet from those who never miss a chance to exploit whatever is of value till the treasure is gone."

"Like what, Doctor?" asked a man from the back row.

She was hoping someone would ask. "I haven't even told you this, yet, Dear," she said, and she showed a picture of an elephant with tusks.

"That's not your elephant," he said.

"No, but it could be her baby's father. Some of them have such tusks. This is a video of me feeding the babies while the mother looks on."

The crowd oohed and ahhed, and the Captain was even more confused about his wife's intentions for this presentation.

"As I was saying, in Africa all the elephants have tusks, and the humans hunt them."

"Why do they want their tusks?"

"They saw them off and then carve them into ornaments and jewelry."

"Doesn't that hurt them?"

"I don't know, but the elephant is a powerful animal, and they'd never put up with it, so they kill them first."

"They kill the animal to steal a bone to make decorations? There must be easier ways to make ornaments? Why are these so valuable?" "Because they are rare. But why would that make them valuable? This is a good lesson in evolution."

"Alpha evolution!" announced a teenager. "Because only powerful men--physically powerful with guns or financially powerful enough to afford the ivory--can secure them for the female, and she unconsciously trusts that he will be rich and powerful enough to provide for their children so she wants to mate with him?"

"Good answer," she said, "but the female doesn't necessarily think any of this consciously. Like our Alphas, she may just find the powerful man irresistible and have no clue why."

"But why isn't that overridden by compassion for the animal?"

"Oh, they lost compassion in evolution."

"Completely?"

"Most didn't lose it completely; but like the Alpha, they only feel it for selected people. Like our Alphas, they don't concern themselves with what their immediate gain is costing others. Though not all humans are like this, the exploiters seem to have greater numbers and seem more ruthless in their aggression. We would hope they could use words to bridge the gap between the two groups, but they recently experienced a great failure in the form of a war. As we know, there is no greater horror than speaking out about ones suffering and having it fall on indifferent ears. They are losing an opportunity few species have. The waste is terrible, but we can't save them."

A mother tuned to the Captain and asked, "Could we make a home here and defend ourselves if they attacked?"

"You would think so. It isn't very densely populated, but they are very territorial, and each inch of space belongs to someone, so if we settled, some human would come to evict us."

"But when they saw were were doing no harm, surely they'd let us be," argued a young Beta mother.

"You would think so," she said, "but they have weapons, even nuclear weapons---"

"---but surely they wouldn't use them on---"

"---And they've already used them on enemy civilians."

"'Enemy civilians': What does that even mean?" said the mother. "Bombing doesn't clothe their child, feed their wives, build their village. What does it serve?"

"It serves their rage. That's all," he said.

"No," said the mother. "This place is not safe for children."

"So, we will leave, and the Alphas may come here and decide to follow us."

"No earthling will know why we left or where we went. Maybe the Alphas will think we perished," suggested the same mother.

"That would be great for us, not so great for Earth."

A young father rose to speak. "Actually, this is good news. The Alphas sent us here, and they are on their way, and we really don't want to see them in any new world, so we'll move on. If we were to stay, we'd soon be living under Alpha control again."

The Captain surveyed the faces in the room. He saw the Betas shake their heads, each looking determined and grave. They would not stay.

"How much time do we have?" asked the father.

"By Earth clocks, decades. By the clocks traveling at light speed, days. We have identified some class M planets that might be hospitable, and after everyone's had a tour of Earth, we'll be off to greener pastures. Any suggestions, folks?"

The passengers filled the meeting with many suggestions, as smart people with a lot of time on their hands are wont to do. All of the suggestions were carefully noted. Then they turned down the lights for the "Einstein and Carlos video," while the command staff retired to their meeting room, though they would hear the giggles when the professor came onscreen.

The first item on the agenda concerned their next destination. The Alphas rarely allowed Betas a voice, so they could not resist speaking up; and after much discussion, they decided to take the Captain's recommendation.

Second, the Captain wanted their suggestions on how to disguise their escape route. The Captain kept asking for ideas until his engineer suggested, "Let's warp in one direction, come out of warp, drift off the trajectory, and coast into the planned coordinates.

Backtracking, they might find the warp signature eventually, but it won't be easy, and it will buy us some time," he said.

The Captain smiled at the suggestion, leading his wife to suspect he'd thought of this idea but wanted someone else to suggest it. The navigator then showed them a chart with the next closest M-class planet they'd found in their search.

"If it isn't suitable, this search could take forever," complained the engineer, probably worried how long his engines would hold up.

"But the more places we visit, the harder it will be for them to find us," she said with a smile.

"But if they do find us?" asked the Chief of Security.

The Captain answered, "If we are in a position of strength, they will bargain with us. If not, they will take what they want and let us live if they have some use for us, as always."

"What about the repercussions for our attempt at evasion?" asked the Chief.

The Captain answered, "The responsible party will be punished."

"That's you."

"It is."

"Part of your punishment will be the suffering of your family."

"It won't come to that." The Captain said it in a way that did not invite further discussion.

Chapter 6

When the Beta shuttles listened in on the humans below in West Texas, they heard a twelve year-old boy who wasn't interested in farming, who wanted to learn how to reproduce the colors painted on the Texas sky, who couldn't help from thinking differently, who believed in his heart that the world was created in six days as he'd been taught, but couldn't believe it with his mind. They heard his family tell him he was a sinner who insulted his family and turned his back on God.

They gathered around their viewers and watched the drama as if it were a serial on the radio, since the earthlings didn't have television yet. As he was packing up to leave home, his dog--an old border collie who'd been given to him when he was a young boy--kept sitting in his suitcase so he couldn't pack his clothes.

As the Chief Medical Officer passed the family recreation lounge, she heard a child ask, "How does the dog know he's leaving home?"

So she stuck her head in and watched the dog removing the boy's clothes and his sketch pads from the suitcase.

"I have to go," the boy told the dog, and I can't take care of you on the road. I won't even be able to hitch a ride with you along, but I'll come back for you, Laddie. I will."

She watched as the dog licked the boy's tears and tried to follow him out to the road, but the boy shut the door behind him and lugged his bag out to the country road and walked into the night. She could still hear the dog's howl as she hurried from the lounge.

Then, one spring night in west Texas around the town of Marfa, the citizens were treated to a light show. Circles of light descended from the heavens in formation and then sprayed in all directions. If they could have followed each, the spectators might have noticed that each light circle landed on a butte, one of the towers of stone that rise from the plains and flatten off due to an erosion-resistant cap of cooled lava. If they could have watched from above, they would have seen each saucer dump one of the tracking devices that the Alphas had hidden aboard the mother-ship.

After performing this last task, they filled the shuttles with crew who wanted view the planet. Their tour provoked a cluster of UFO sightings:

One of their favorite tourist destinations was a peninsula which looked like a hand. On May 25, 1948 three shuttles were conducting a tour when two Air Force officers reported a UFO sighting. As soon as they realized they'd been sighted, the shuttle veered portside.

A fourth shuttle circled that farm in West Texas until the collie came out to work in the pasture. The collie perked up its ears and began to bark.

"He has good hearing," the Captain commented. "Why are we doing this. Tell me again."

"Because somehow we've missed getting to know this creature, and he might be the best this planet has to offer. But that's not why we're kidnapping him."

"Good. Why are we?"

"Because he's alone and heart-broken."

"Good enough!" he said and landed outside of view from the house.

"Laddie!" she called.

After that, they tried visiting at night but the Beta tourists complained that they couldn't see anything interesting, so on July 24, they gave everybody one final look. In broad daylight they took the mothership down near a gulf almost due south of the hand-shaped peninsula so all the crew and passengers could bid good-bye.

When a native airplane approached on a collision course, the mothership fired its thrusters and elevated away while the passengers waved good-bye from the double row of portholes. Once out of Earth's atmosphere, they unfurled the sails and rose perpendicular to the solar system's axis to find their point of ignition into warp drive.

"I think you are going to be very grateful to me one of these days," she said with a smile.

"I'm grateful to you everyday," he answered with a leer.

"But not for my brain."

"That too, sometimes"

"For my amazing judgment or maybe intuition?"

'In that case, I might need an example."

"I knew it. I'm just another unappreciated wife!"

"Quit fishing for compliments. What miracle have to performed now?"

"You know how you like to criticize Carlos?"

"Your opossum?"

"No, the other Carlos, the one we brought from Mexico after our wild weekend in Tijuana."

Silence

"Yes, that Carlos."

Silence

"Well, if you insist on my telling you, do you remember that he scratched my hand?"

"Vaguely. How is it?"

"It got infected."

"I'm not surprised. We have no resistance to earth's germs. Let me see." He looks. "I don't see anything. Why are you complaining?"

"I'm not complaining. I'm bragging. Here is how it looked two days ago," and she showed him a photo of a red, swollen palm.

"I never noticed. I'm sorry, Love."

"Thank you, but I wasn't going for sympathy."

"That looks nasty. How did you cure it?"

"I didn't. Carlos did. He felt guilty for what he'd done and licked it. Do you know what Carlos ate back on earth?"

"Nothing fierce, smart, or fast."

"Nope, the Professor told us: garbage, bugs, and dead things."

"First he gave you an infection; and then his nasty mouth cured it with homegrown antibiotics? Is that why you brought him along?"

"Of course not. That's no more the reason to bring him than to bring you. You're both cute and sweet but," she said, swirling her index finger in curls noodling up from her brain to the cosmos, "then I suspected that Carlos was going to be a little antibiotic factory. He could be a big help if he can do as well with new germs we find wherever it is we land."

"Bugs, garbage, and dead things," he said and walked away muttering something about working with family members. Taking out his communicator, he connected the Chief.

"What is it, Captain?"

"I called to tell you that I appreciate your work this the animals."

"Thank you, Sir."

"And with my wife."

Silence

"And to tell you that sometimes it *is* difficult."

"Yes, Sir. Thank you, Sir. But she was right, Sir."

"That's the burden we share, we men. Would you please stop with the *sir*'s now?"

Chapter 7

Meanwhile, as the Betas were warping to their next M class

planet, the Alphas had arrived at Earth. Their first order of business

sent them looking for the Betas. They began by searching for the

signals sent out by tracking devices they'd hidden on the mothership

and shuttles.

When residents of Marfa in West Texas saw the lighted discs

zooming from butte to butte as they had a few decades later, they

would say, "They're lookin for that ship that crashed in '47," but

they'd've been wrong. They couldn't have known that the saucers

operated by Alphas in the '70's were trying to understand why their

instruments were telling them that the Betas were on those barren

buttes. One Alpha shuttle circled Wright-Patterson Air Force Base east

of Dayton, Ohio over and over but could see nothing on the ground

that resembled a shuttle craft.

Finding no evidence of the Betas, the new visitors made a quick

study of the Earthlings. Thus began a period of saucer sightings on

Earth, a generation of kidnapping victims, rarely believed but spawning legends and at least one popular television show which led the humans to think the Alphas who were controlling this invasion were small, hairless, grey people, whereas, in truth (1) only the male Betas are hairless and (2) the Betas who did the kidnapping and probing of victims were merely the medical personnel of the Alpha-operated mothership which hovered behind the moon.

Having no interest in the humans, themselves, and seeing that global warming was progressing apace, the Alphas had no interest in the planet either, so they departed without ever bothering to introduce themselves to their hosts.

During this brief period, the Betas never gave up their fear that the Alphas were following them. So, they were not surprised when they received a transmission from a ship identical to theirs.

"Prepare for our arrival!" ordered its Commanding officer.

When his kidnappers passed the word on to Laddie, along with a treat, he seemed quite happy at the news. Carlos, on the other hand, remained grouchy and stinky.

The couple debated donning their flight suits for the invasion but couldn't bring themselves to give up the simple smock that all the Betas now wore. So, when the shuttles landed and the Alpha Captain gazed down the gangplank, he saw a sparse crowd of little, grey Betas, all seeming to be wearing pajamas.

First down the ramp came the soldiers, and they formed two lines for the Alpha General who had seen them off some years before. He ducked his head at the shuttle door, took his time navigating the gangplank and approached the couple at the other end of the lines.

Why do those soldiers stand on either side of him? Do they protect him from us? What can we do? Are they reminders that he has power and can give orders to people? wondered the thin, grey long-haired Beta standing next to a border collie with a sock in his mouth and her mate, a bald man in a smock,

"What's this?" he scoffed the General through curled lips.

"Greetings, General. I'm sure you remember my wife, so I assume you are asking about a recent addition to our family. This is Laddie. He won't say much with that sock in his mouth."

"You told him to 'Put a sock in it, did you?'" he said and then howled at his own joke. "Well, let's see what he has to say?" and he stretched out his hand to the sock.

Naturally, Laddie wouldn't open his mouth, as much as he wanted to bite the greenish hand, so he clenched tight and growled. The General tugged and laughed; and when most dog-lovers would relent, the Alpha persisted in tugging till he had almost lifted the dog off the ground.

The Chief Medical Officer officer squeezed the former Captain's hand as he was about to warn the General and stopped him in mid "General, I d---."

All of the Betas watched with interest as the General bent over and reached his right hand toward the border collie's sock-filled mouth. Grasping Laddie's lower jaw with his right, his left reached over the snout, pressed between the dog's lips and pulled apart the jaws.

Events then sped up: The sock came loose; both grabbed at it, General and collie alike. Intentional or not, the General's hand ended up in Laddie's mouth; skin was broken; blood oozed; apologies abounded.

While the Beta husband handed the sock back to Laddie, the General said, "Don't worry. It's just a flesh wound. I've suffered worse wounds than this combating our world's enemies. "

"Superficial, but maybe not very clean," the doctor muttered. "You'll want to wash that off. Their bites can be dirty."

"I've never seen him do that before, General," said the Captain.

His wife gave him a quizzical look, thinking, *What are you saying? That dog will bite anyone who tries to take his sock.*

They guided the dignitaries to a group of buildings the Betas had built for themselves out of a cellulose foam, creating a light-weight but insulating material that could take any shape the occupant wished. His wife excused herself to, in her words, "ready some native food."

After the Medical Officer was out of earshot, the General muttered, "I thought you would have done more with the place. This looks like a primitive village."

Simple, General, but hardly primitive, thought the Beta physicist.

First she visited the kitchen to collect some garbage. Then she went to find Carlos, a bigger Carlos than she'd first met. Though his head hadn't grown much, his body had swelled to terrier size but fatter and rounded back with spines of wiry hair sticking out in various directions. He scratched along on long-fingered paws, built more for digging and picking through garbage than running. (She'd never seen Carlos run.) His whiskers had grown longer, but they were more sparse and did not invite petting, so love Carlos though she did, she did not bother him with physical affection. Instead, she fed him fruit from her hand and explained his job. "All I want you to do is sniff and drool," she said, and Carlos did. He sniffed and then drooled, and she collected that drool with the intent to test it for antibodies she could collect and apply to the General's wound to combat whatever microbes might have been in Laddie's mouth. At least, that was her intention.

Back at the styrofoam building the Captain was telling the General, "We observed on Earth how common the urge to dominate other life forms must be, and we understand its appeal, but it's never been our goal. Being the dominated has been our past, but it won't be our future, at least not those of us on this planet. This universe came with an expiration date. You will want to pursue your nature in the days you have left, so if you insist on having this planet, we'll look elsewhere for our new home. We won't go on living as you do, as if there were a way to win, a way to live forever. The best any of us can do is live in harmony, but you don't care about that. You like the illusion of victory even when there is no real competition." Then he raised his glass to the General.

"We could just force you aboard against your will. I'm curious why you haven't taken more defensive precautions for our arrival."

"We've made precautions against inhospitality," he joked, reaching for the pitcher that sat between them. "Would you like a homemade tea? It's not like that on your home planet, but it has an interesting bite. This green goo can be used for sweetener.

"So that world is ours now. I suspect you think of this world as 'yours,' and not ours. Well, regardless, we are leaving some Alphas to administer, and you and your officers are coming back with us, those of you who do not protest too hard. The most resistant will, I'm afraid, briefly regret their stubbornness and then pass quickly into oblivion. We can import a thousand more of your feeble brethren to do our bidding."

"I suspect that it gives you a self-satisfied pride to sit back and survey all you've conquered. Conquest doesn't do that for us. We look at it and wonder what you have ever built that is an improvement. So, we find it increasingly difficult to enjoy our lives in your world. That is why we decided to stop cooperating. I think as much as you would like the old 'us' back, you will be better off without the new 'us.'"

At that point in this civilization-altering conversation, the Beta Captain's wife entered, leading Carlos on a leash.

"What is that abomination?" asked the General.

"General, please meet Carlos. Carlos, this is the General. Don't be afraid he won't kill you."

"Is that creature native to this planet?"

"No, sadly, General, we have found no other Carlos here, only on Earth, but that is good for you because Carlos shares germs with the dog who bit you a few minutes ago."

"I don't see why that is good for me," he grumbled.

"Because his drool might disinfect that bite. I can ask Carlos to lick the wound, or I can dab some of his drool onto the wound, whichever you'd prefer."

"That's not going to happen! What is going to happen instead is that you two and your officers are going to join me on my shuttle. My soldiers are going to enforce Alpha rule here and get these Betas clearing this land and building a suitable dwellings for the arrival of large numbers of our dying planet's citizens."

"That's disappointing news, isn't it Love?" asked the husband.

"Very. Did you offer the General some tea? Though I don't think it will help with the infection."

"I am sending the two of you off to the mother ship. You have five minutes to pack a bag. Sergeant, escort them to and from their quarters, and get rid of that stinking creature."

"Be nice to Carlos," she said. "If you don't like his smell now, you really won't like it if he gets scared."

While the Betas were packing, the General tried to communicate with the mothership, but had trouble reaching the computer. So, he called the ship Captain's communicator.

"Sorry, General, the computer seems to have gone down. We can't seem to diagnose the problem."

The General radioed his Sergeant and ordered, "Bring them here!" The Sergeant yanked his two prisoners hard enough to please the General, if he'd been there to witness the display of domination, and sent them stumbling in the General's direction.

"What have you done!" he asked.

"I'd have to ask our AI, General. I left him some general instructions. He may have improvised."

"Answer my question!" growled the General.

"AI?"

"Yes, Captain."

"Would you update us on the situation aboard the Alpha mothership?"

"Certainly, Sir. The Alpha computer and I have gotten to know each other. We've done some new things with programming, Captain."

"How nice."

"Tell me what's going on aboard my ship, or I will kill the Captain and his wife."

"That sounds like the General, Sir. I don't like his tone. Should I tell his computer to blow up the ship?"

"I'm afraid you are upsetting my AI, General. You're going to have to tone it down a little." Before the General could order him shot, he went on, "Please give the General an update, AI."

"Okay." He sounded disappointed. "I've taught him to tell jokes. Here, listen. Go ahead, computer."

"Have you heard the one about the General who couldn't get back on his own ship?" said a voice.

"That's not my computer!" insisted the General. "It has a female voice."

"That was my idea," said AI. "I kind of like it. It goes better with the less Alpha-centered value system that I programmed in."

"Value system! It's a goddam computer. It doesn't have a value system!"

"Sorry, Captain. The General seems upset. You said I should add whatever might help his computer follow your orders to have the

Beta crew take over his ship and forbid him to board until you and he have reached an agreement on the fate of the planet."

"I don't believe you!" said the General.

"Show him, AI," and the screen showed Betas crew training weapons on the skeleton crew of Alpha prisoners.

AI prattled on, "I hope the jokes aren't offensive. She tells them like a child because she doesn't really understand them. I find it quite amusing. There might still be some bugs in my programming."

"Knock knock," said the Alpha computer.

"Lower the sound, please, AI," said the Captain.

"As you wish, Captain."

"Here's your situation, General. You are massively outnumbered. You can't gain re-entry to your ship without our assistance. It is now programed to cause the least suffering possible to all beings, and AI has input data concerning the subjective experience of various life forms other than Alphas, not just Betas, but other sentient beings, like Laddie--which experience fear, love, protectiveness, sadness, loss."

"Especially the elephants," she whispered. "AI likes the elephants a lot."

The General said, "How can a computer like anything?

"He really struggles with illogic. He sees no reason why you would be the center of the universe. He doesn't value you any more than Carlos."

"Who's Carlos?"

"See, you don't even remember his name. And he sort of has a sense of humor--AI, not Carlos--in that he likes to find and delete illogical things. He appreciates tight, economical reasoning, and Alpha-centeredness isn't such a thought process. He likes identifying invalid first-premises. So, while he would prefer not to exterminate you, if you give him a choice between us and our pets and the creatures he is cataloguing on this planet, you will rank a distant-- How many is it now, AI?"

"6.309479 millionth and counting," sings AI.

The Captain muttered, "I've never noticed before, but male and female speech patterns differ."

"And?" asked his wife.

"AI's become pretty female, strangely female."

"It's strange that he sounds female?" she asked while the General looked on, speechless.

"No, he sounds like a strange female."

"Is that a problem?"

"No, but why would it happen?"

"You gave him a Beta woman's perspective. We're---"

"---Rubbish!" barked the General, and he ordered his troops back onto the shuttle. Within the hour, they zoomed off to the mother ship.

Listening in through the linked computers, the Captain and his First Mate heard the ship's computer refuse entry to the mothership. Instead, it ordered them to leave all the weapons behind and return to the planet unarmed.

Aided by hand-held transporter devices, the exchange of arms for Betas continued till Beta crew and weapons had landed on the ground in the shuttles, and unarmed Alphas were aboard the mothership.

As the General readied to embark, he commented, "If I understand you correctly, you have lured us here after delaying us at Earth so you would have time to arrange our Waterloo. If I know you, you would even allow us a place here if each of us would become one of your pets. I will report what I am able to see here, and they might want to send an expedition, though the apparent absence of a compliant workforce is a drawback. Since the planet doesn't have much to offer us, I don't begrudge you your refuge. You have your dreams. We have ours. And in the end, we all fade to darkness, so what does it all matter?"

The Captain answered, "You aren't without an awareness of the suffering you cause, are you? I was never sure."

"No, of course we are aware. We have to be. As you've shown, a resentful workforce represents a security risk."

"So, you notice; and I suspect you care about the suffering of some others, other Alphas."

"Care about the suffering of others? Yes, but not just Alphas. The suffering or displeasure of anyone I am responsible for alerts me to trouble, and I grow concerned and seek to solve the problem."

"Do you ever feel compassion?"

"I'm not sure what you mean."

"How about sadness? Have you ever felt sad?"

"When my mother died. As she was dying, I did feel impatient with her suffering."

"Impatient with her?"

"No, not that heartless. I wanted to end her suffering. I could empathize with her physical pain and her fear. And I felt like I would miss her."

"Did you?"

"Not much, really. This must seem strange to you."

"No, we've studied reptiles."

"I suppose you mean that as an insult, but I take none. The snake is very efficient and successful. But I think the colonial insect is a better analogy. They work together, do a job, sacrifice for the collective. I'm sure we'd conquer the universe if it weren't for time."

"And dark energy."

"Yes, I've always felt resentful toward the tendency of things to fall apart. So, you see, we each follow our inherited nature. Your compassion is both a strength and a weakness, but your brain is your great treasure."

"It's a tool, but I live in my heart."

Finally, the General was beamed aboard. As the mothership neared position to engage warp drive, they received a transmission from him:

"May you enjoy the time you have left. If we can, we will return and conquer you."

"I know. See you soon, then."

"Not me, but others."

"Why not you, General?"

"Because it appears you were right about the dog bite. I should have accepted that opossum's drool."

After communication had been terminated, the General asked his crewman if he'd successfully hidden the receiver for the transporter on the planet.

"Yessir."

Then the General died.

"Too bad he died. That'll bring them back. It upsets their sense of order that Betas would win," said the former Chief Surgeon and current immunologist and vet. "But they'll be back as soon as they've done an autopsy and identified the bacteria."

"If they can find us with their log erased," said her husband.

"You erased their log?"

"Not me exactly--I was never aboard."

"AI did it?"

"He liked doing it."

"Liked?"

"He doesn't agree with the Alpha-AI's premises--dominance by his creators, suppressions of inferior races, all the opposite of how we programmed our AI. So he liked sneaking in and erasing the log."

"How will they get back? Have you killed them, my husband?"

"I might have if I weren't your husband, but I asked AI to infect it with a virus that would erase the log after they arrived home and came out of warp."

"They'll make it back here someday if they want to bad enough."

"We'll take our chances. What choice do we have? All this building of wealth. For what? How much more do we need? How many planets shall we destroy?"

"You're preaching to the choir again, Dear," she told him.

"Yes, let's call the congregation together. I need to address everyone, but what do we call ourselves? Are we still Betas? The Earthlings lived on Earth. What shall we call this planet?"

"When the natives appear, we can ask them," she said.

"You don't think we're alone?" he challenged.

"I doubt it. The planet has all the conditions for evolution to proceed, but we see no humanoids. How is that possible?"

"You can ask them at the meeting what they want to be called."

"Me?"

"I think you should do the talking."

"I think you're right."

The immunologist stood on a tree stump, facing several hundred of her neighbors and informed them, "My fellow citizens, our would-be Lord died of a simple earthly bacterial infection delivered to him by Laddie, simple but virulent if one lacks Earth's resistance. Laddie's bite should not be a problem for any of us if we don't try to steal his sock. As for Carlos, I notice none of you seem particularly interested in touching him, but that's okay. His feelings will not be hurt. As a matter of fact, he prefers it that way. If you do try to touch him, he will faint from fear and begin to smell like a dead animal."

"Ooh, yuck," said one of the crowd.

Someone else asked, "Why did you bring him?"

"Well, I like him, but I also brought him for his antibodies. He's a member of the medical staff now."

The children laughed.

"My husband thinks I have 'the mind of a child,' as he likes to say."

Chapter 8

By this time ten years had passed on Earth, and the artist, now a young man, returned home to visit his family in West Texas. He was happily struggling as an painter; and the fact that in his pocket he had money from selling drawings and paintings softened his father's disapproval. He started introduce him around as "my son, the arteest." The only fly in the ointment, or burr under the saddle, since this was, after all, West Texas had to do with Laddie's mysterious disappearance.

He lay down on his bed and slipped his hands under his pillow to support his head, and there he found a sock. He recognized the sock. Laddie used to hide this sock and its mate from him and sleep with them. The sock crinkled in his grip, so he stretched his fingers inside and found a note:

"Laddie is fine and misses you and carries your other sock with him everyplace. By the time you get this note, many years will have passed, but we assure you we have never washed your sock; Laddie has never stopped loving you; and don't worry: We are taking care of him. Friends."

Shortly after, in galactic terms, a ship appeared from nowhere above the unnamed M class planet and looked perfect on their screen. When his face appeared, the cheerful, handsome Captain explained, "We've been monitoring events below and see you are being threatened by another race. We will provide any help you may need."

The immunologist listened as her husband responded in a surprisingly unfriendly way:

"It depends on how you plan to help and if you want something in return, and what that might be."

"You have many questions," the ship's captain said cheerfully.

"Yes, you might start by explaining what you are and what you want."

"What we are? You can see what we are."

"Yes and no. Your image is very clear on our computer screen, but your ship is not visible to our telescopes or any of our light-sensitive instruments. The computer says you are very close. You should even be visible from the naked eye---"

"---Yet you don't see us."

"No, we don't."

"And yet here we are."

"My computer tells me you are not what you seem, not a ship, not a multicelled being. In fact, we can find no chemical signal for you at all."

"What could I be?"

"I'm afraid, Captain, you are just a transmission, and your source is a master of illusion."

Now she began to have her own suspicions about these unusually good manners. The visitor teased her husband:

"So, where did I come from?"

"I don't know your source, but you did not arrive through three-dimensional space. You must have arrived via wormhole."

"Bingo!"

"Most wormholes aren't very big. Perhaps you aren't as big as you seem."

"Very good. Well, size sometimes doesn't matter. But I'm forgetting my manners. Let me introduce---"

"No. No. No, I extended no invitation, just in case you need one to gain entrance, as legend suggests."

"Legend? How can I put you at ease? Do you wish to see my face as it really is?"

"No, I'm not inviting any relationship of any kind."

"I can show you anyway, you know."

"Of course. In fact, I suspect we have seen you everywhere we've gone. Maybe you can appear and disrupt, but you can't get what you want without an invitation."

"And what do I want?"

"I don't know, but let me speculate. Considering your size, perhaps you only wish us to join your crew in the seven hidden dimensions, touring the subatomic universe."

"My, my, you have quite an imagination. Where did you hear such stories?"

"Nowhere, I'm just fishing."

"Fishing?"

"Trolling for clues to reveal the truth."

"I can show you eternity. I offer you escape from this dying universe."

"Ah, we're dying, but you know the universe isn't. Matter and energy aren't dying. They're just recycling themselves. I don't know what happens to you during this period, but I imagine being essentially bodiless, you'll do fine."

"Do you ever wonder what's become of your dead relatives and loved ones?"

"Are you you inviting us to an early death by traveling to visiting our dead relatives and loved ones?"

The Captain realized he had invited the ship's Captain to show him more, and immediately there appeared on the screen the Captain's mother and the assassinated Gandhi.

"If you join us, you'll be in good company," said the smiling Captain.

Then, seeing her father join them on screen, the First Mate burst, "Poppa! What are you doing there?"

"No consorting with the crew till you've signed on with the crew," said the Captain on the screen.

Standing beside him, her father smiled and beckoned.

"Off!" ordered the Captain. "Did you get a coordinates?" he asked.

AI answered, "No, he has no time-space location; yet he is close, somehow. I'm babbling. How can an AI make no sense?"

"AI, can you try to explain?"

"I can tell you what he isn't. You are correct that he was not here in our three dimensional space."

"No physical body, no actual ship, then."

"Correct, Captain, all virtual, just a transmission, as you guessed, though that allows the possibility that the ship exists in our time and three-dimensional space on the other side of the wormhole. The the wormhole is undetectably small, photon sized. We can only infer its existence."

"I wonder how he spotted us. What drew him here?"

AI answered, "I can't answer that , but it appears he tailored his image for you and the First Mate. Something attracted him to you two."

"Am I your first mate, dear?" she asked.

"You almost were," he assured her. "Threat analysis, AI."

"Severe, Sir. It isn't harvesting beings, themselves. Bodies couldn't navigate a photon-sized wormhole."

"The presence of an image of your father suggests it probed you psyche for an important relationship, Love."

"But why me?" she asked.

"Good question," said the Captain. "You were very glad to see your father. Assume that there is, or once was, a being at the other end of the wormhole. Perhaps this creature would have some interest in the feelings we derive from oxytocin. He can't lure beings through a wormhole so small, but he could transmit all your chemical information in two dimensions and then reconstruct it in 3D to make oxytocin."

"Sure," she said, "but he'd only have to do that once, and then he could synthesize oxytocin, himself, and shoot himself up? What are the chances this is his maiden voyage? For that matter, what are the chances that he has a nervous system that would react like we do to oxytocin?"

The Captain thought aloud, "So, what might be happening here? Something appears on our screen. It looks like a ship, but it isn't a ship. It's not corporeal at all, only an image received by computers. AI says maybe this 'ship' and its 'crew' are just a signal transmitted in two dimensions, but we don't know how it's sent. It very well might have come through a wormhole to some sort of receiver at our end."

"That's me!" said AI.

"And since it contains information about our dead relatives, it may be trying to hijack something about attachment and loss."

"I don't like him very much. Why would he do that? Not for the oxytocin, not for our bliss."

The Captain responds, "Maybe he was stimulated by the connection itself; and by inserting himself in the process of reuniting dead father and live daughter, he momentarily felt the vibrations of the string itself."

"You saw what he did when I recognized my father. He moved the focus to himself, coming between me and my dad, and you could see the effect it had on me: I yearned."

"Yes! He must be interested in the energy that forms our attachments," answered the Captain.

She replied, "Why would our emotional attachments need energy? We need only chemicals, like oxytocin, to feel attachment. This guys shows up with no body and two ghosts. What do we know about relationships with dead people?"

"Of course, communication requires energy, but we have no instrument that can detect the energy which transmits 'extra-sensory' information."

"What are you talking about?"

"We don't know how people communicate psychically, but they do. It is especially common at, or right after, the moment of death. What does that suggest about how it is happening?"

"Mmm," she hummed. "I wouldn't know, but I know how your think. If ESP signals were traveling through regular space, we'd've detected them by now, so the signals have to burrow through the other dimensions like the strings connecting entangled photons."

"I never knew you paid any attention when I talk about physics."

"I try not to, but sometimes I can't shut it out."

"Well, that's exactly what I suspect about ESP, ghost sightings, and the near-death reports of souls travelling through a tunnel."

"What? So that's why people see visions of going through a dark passageway in near-death experiences?" she asked.

"Those dark passageways may be real," he answered. "What would a wormhole look like to a brain as it is losing its electric field and its body is decaying? "

"You think there's really a tunnel? It's not the hallucination of a dying brain?"

"No, conversations with recently dead people are very common, and why would so many creatures, even Alphas and Earthlings, have such experiences? The universe looks straight and big, but wormholes shorten the distance. Throughout spacetime entanglement through these wormholes link particles. So, two entangled particles can be connected by strings which seem far apart in 3D but are close in 2D. Anyway," he said with a shrug, "the folding of space takes some getting used to, but once you can accept it, the harder question is why space seems so large in our three dimensions. Maybe Professor Einstein guessed right that just by chance light can travel in the big three spatial dimensions, and our vision follows light, so the line of sight seems straight; and the distances, large. We can separate two entangled photons by miles of space, but from their perspective, they remain side-by-side because in very small dimensions, wormholes fold space in a way that makes no common sense."

"I know the theory," she said, "but I never thought I'd have to take it seriously. Here's why I don't like to talk to you about this stuff. First, I have to entertain the possibility that something lives on after we die."

"At least for a little while."

"Right, a soul."

"It's been called that."

"And you are saying it's a particle like a photon or a graviton."

"I'm a physicist. What can I say? I expect real things to follow the rules."

"And the rules are equations," she said. "And these 'spiritons' may be linked with other 'spiritons' and as the person dies, his 'spiriton' can travel through wormholes which the almost-dead person can watch."

"Makes more sense to me than---"

"Wait, I'm not done. I haven't gotten to the weird part yet. As the soul particle is following his string up the tunnel, he may get to the end and meet someone he's attached to even though that person died years ago and thousands of light years away?"

"You have questions I can't answer. How do they exist without a functioning brain? I don't know. So far, it's seemed like matter can be neither created nor destroyed, but where do it go after leaving the body? I don't know. If there are individual souls, is there a Great Spirit, a God? Is there there a physical embodiment of Good and Evil, not just harmful beings like the Alphas, but pure, Evil? What is the composition of the soul? I don't know. I can't answer any of that because whatever I propose to exist, it hasn't been measured in our four, big dimensions."

"But you are suggesting that the attachment between loved ones is literal, physical."

"As a hypothetical, yes."

"I'm going to pin you down. Are you saying that there really exists a soul to entangle?" she asked.

"It depends on what you mean. Is there a non-physical essence that lives forever?" says the Captain. "As a physicist, I'd say, 'No, there isn't anything non-physical. On the other hand, there is obviously more to this universe than meets the eye. We know people can be psychically or emotionally linked even though they are far away and out of sight. It's reasonable to hypothesize that some energy--therefore, some string--literally connects them and bends time and space just as entanglement can. So, when we feel attached to people, there may be actual strings of energy connecting us in one of the seven smaller dimensions where we can't detect them."

"So signing on to that ship, do I have a chance to reconnect with my father?"

"There's the rub, Love. No, I don't think that *is* your father. When you tried to tell him about your attachments--to me, to Laddie, to Carlos--when you described the 'possum's hand-like paws with their fingers and long 'nails,' the rat-like tail you find so appealingly ugly, the whiskers around his snout, the horrible smell that protects him from predators---"

---"Ohh, he's so cute! I didn't think you noticed."

---"I noticed. Yuck! These things, my lovely wife, you and your weird father shared. But when you told his image on the viewing screen, he remained expressionless. The camera shifted to their captain, who continued to preach about his love for you two. Here, I'll replay it for you":

"'I desire nothing more in this lifetime than bringing lost souls together forever, where they belong,' preached the ship's Captain, while all that can be seen of your father is his left arm. See, he keeps talking about love and bringing you together, but he is completely drowning you out, preventing a connection, and worst of all, the supposed father does not respond at all to you, his daughter. He didn't lean into the camera and say, 'Hey, what color was Carlos' tail?' My conclusion: that 'father' was just a face hijacked from your memory. His essence was absent. He didn't even respond emotionally when you began to cry about missing him or wanting to help the beasts who need you like Carlos, Laddie, and me and your unborn children. The captain covered for your 'father' by talking into the camera---"

"If I treated him as if he had just died, and mourned him and created my own little Hell---"

Said AI, "That idea leads to an even more malevolent possibility. Maybe the opposite is true. Maybe he--let's just call him Satan for fun--started out hijacking bliss until he learned to make it himself and them he found himself feeling pleasure when other beings suffered from the feelings brought by loss--the grief, the misery of losing oxytocin. He has the capacity to create hell--a constant reminder of loss, and endless repetition."

"What could be more evil?" she said. "In the process he creates a Hell of loss and longing for someone like myself who wants to reunite with her father."

"We have heard of such beings. So have the earthlings," muttered the Captain quietly. "You've convinced me he isn't after the oxytocin, itself. These images of our loved ones are pretty lame. Maybe he wants the opposite--oxytocin depletion. Maybe he wants to stimulate mourning and he feeds off our misery."

"So, Satan's a pornographer of despair," she said angrily.

"What?"

"He gets pleasure being present, watching, when people mourn."

"That is strangely consistent with our images of Hell, souls separated from God and mourning," he mused. "And since he wouldn't have our chemistry or wouldn't rely on chemistry, he may respond directly to the strings. He may be attracted their vibrations the way ants are attracted to electricity."

"That's a weird analogy."

"Maybe it's literally similar and not an analogy at all. When some ants are electrocuted, they wave, or *flag*, their abdomen, or *gaster*, in the air to release pheromones that, in turn, attract other worker ants."

"Ants attracted by death."

"Satan is like a very tiny electrician with a gigantic food supply of us ants who cling to our dead and dying fellow ants."

AI adds, "That's very poetic, but we are hypothesizing that Satan resonates with these strings. He can't reproduce the strings, but he can hijack them, collect their pattern and play it back for himself in the privacy of his own theater. So maybe there is a live being at the other end getting stimulated by watching what's left of your sadness about losing your father. If he can't watch the real thing live, he can replay it."

"It's like spiritual pornography. His video collection is stored in Hell. When he gets the urge, he plays one of his favorite recordings of human misery and gets off, so to speak," said the Captain.

"That's perverted, horrible, despicable," she objected.

"You thought someone we're calling *Satan* would be otherwise? So, I don't like your plan to mourn. It would be miserable for you, plus the string, the connection between father and daughter, would be excited. If we wants to feel the string vibrate, he will enjoy any interaction you try to have with your father. Instead, let's give him what he doesn't want: If you ignore your father's image, if you act as if you were completely finished with mourning, as if your father were dead and gone, just a memory?---"

"---Me? The woman who had nightmares about lab hamsters suffering? How could I see my father and not mourn?"

"You could do it if you really concentrated on how that was not your father's spirit, just a fake, an impostor."

"Not good enough. My father's still dead. That makes me sad."

"Concentrate on the fact that *the Captain* is an impostor trying to lure you into an abyss where your strongest attachments are stolen by a soul sucker."

"Yes, that might prevent my misery. There's nothing like righteous indignation to drive the blues away. Bring that bastard back! I'm going to give *him* my undivided attention! This's gonna get ugly."

"Hopefully, ugly enough to close an ancient wormhole. AI, can you pull up the picture of her smiling father?"

He showed both of them.

She stared a moment, then closed her eyes and concentrated. Gradually tears slowly crept down her cheeks.

"Can you find the ship?" whispered the Captain.

"I'll see if I can find his trail," said AI.

"Thank you, AI."

"Why do you thank him?" she asked, irritated and sniffling.

"Because he likes to be thanked."

"You mean he's programmed to seek thanks."

"Whatever. One's silicon, one's DNA. What's the difference?" he replied, wondering why they were arguing.

"That's the attitude I need," she said. "I need your emotional distance. That's what will protect my emotional involvement with that zombi."

"You must focus on your contempt for him, not your longing for your father. You must be completely emotionally uninvolved with that imitation of our father."

"Bliss sucker!" she repeated.

A picture of the shiny ship came onscreen.

The Captain told his wife, "So, horrible as it may sound, I think we are seeing a ghost ship, a ship without a crew, fulfilling its program to feed off the relationships between other beings."

"Bliss sucker!" she growled.

The ship crew appeared on the screen; and for an instant, the face of its captain appeared to glow with good-will.

Before turning on the microphone, the Captain announced, "And now we see the image of the person responsible for hijacking from her own memories the image of my wife's dead father. Let's pump that ship with contempt!" and the camera focused on the man who pretended to bring her a father back from the dead. The Beta pressed "send," and the smile on the ship captain's face turned to horror. The ship instantaneously shrunk into a bright dot, and the screen went black.

"Take that! You thought you were so smart, preying on people addicted to love!" laughed the Captain. Then he stopped laughing and said, "I shouldn't be so judgemental, should I, Love?"

"Not if you want to keep your supply of oxytocin," she said with a sweet smile. "Did it work?" Then she thought it through and added, "If it did, we'll never know."

Then the Chief Medical Officer recently identified as the almost-First Mate, suggested that she inform the entire settlement about the encounter in case the shiny ship survived and returned.

Some gathered in the meeting room they'd built. Those with children sat around their video receivers as the familiar, grey face of their First Lady smiled out at them. Describing her encounter with the image of her dead father, she said, "It is inevitable that we all will enter that dimension soon enough, but that shiny ship is no realistic representation of what death is like. Death has no space and time. I will not see my father with a smile frozen onto his face. If we did not manage to drive that soul sucker away forever, you may one day turn on your receivers and see the image that promises to connect you with souls you've lost, but I am sure it will actually introduce to a spirit you don't want to know. That devil isn't my captain of choice. I suspect, my fellow Betas, that he bears some responsibility for the absence of humanoids on this planet."

The settlers had many questions about the visit through the wormhole, but the Captain and the First Mate had little more they could tell. They were alone in their quarters when their viewer turned itself. When they looked up they saw the captain smiling from the bridge of his shining ship, but when he opened his mouth to speak, they heard something different.

In a deep voice he growled, "'Evil spirits'? You call us *evil*, but we are merely disruptive. Disruption is necessary, and emotional bonds are among the most difficult to disrupt. We rue the day a species like you evolved that damned God molecule, as they call it, oxytocin. Bond, Bond, Bond," he chanted like a bass drum. "Things get all clogged up unless those bonds are broken. That's what black holes do, and without the service provided by black holes, things would disperse into eternal night. I'll be back. I can't be denied. Enjoy it while you can." Then they heard static.

After a long silence, she asked, "Is our universe simply going to die?"

"Nah, space-time isn't going to fizzle, unless you mean our particular piece of fabric,' 'cause that'll eventually collide with another universe and explode into a whole new universe. Something goes on forever or how could anything exist at all? What would it have started from? So, somehow we recycle--collide with another universe, retract as the fabric is stretched too far. Something continues existence."

"Something completely new?" she asked. "So this expansion of space--will it stretch the connecting wormholes until all the bonds are broken?"

"You mean if it doesn't collide with another universe first?"

"Could the sinuous tissue of strings start to slow the expansion and pull it all back together?"

"You don't want another big bang, do you?"

"Not really."

"Do you think we'd lose contact in a big bang?"

"Yes, everything would be reconstructed, differently."

"That evil voice has you scared about our future as a couple. Will we stay paired for all time even when our four-dimensional bodies are cold and dead?"

"I would like to think that," she said.

"I think I can find you in a gushing ocean of energy. You'll be the girl dragging an opossum and a dog along on leashes, Love."

"I'm going to punch you," she said to her husband, her delicate hand in a fist, ready to strike him; though never before having hit anyone, ever, it was bent in a way that would only result in a broken wrist if she were to punch someone.

The thought of her ever trying to hurt a loved one wouldn't release him till his face hurt from smiling. And he leaned back on the chair in which the receiver was hidden, the device that would permit an Alpha to be electronically transmitted to the planet.

To be continued...

Made in United States
Orlando, FL
29 November 2024

54634571R00070